# RICHARD & LINDA

*New York Times* #1 bestselling authors of *Teaching Your Children Values* and creators of the Joy School curriculum

# JOY SCHOOL

22 STORIES TO TEACH
CHILDREN JOY FROM HONESTY,
SERVICE, GOALS, SHARING,
CARING FOR THE EARTH,
UNIQUENESS, AND MORE!

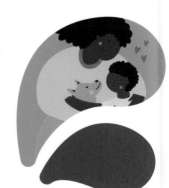

Illustrated by Olga Zakharova

### SAD-OR-HAPPY STORIES

Some of the stories in this book are split into two storylines: the top half of the page shows how poor choices can bring unhappiness, and the bottom half of the page shows how good choices can bring joy. When reading these stories, cover up half of each page at a time and help kids compare the different outcomes.

# CONTENTS

# INTRODUCTION

*The Joy School Story*

EVEN BEFORE THEY WERE #1 *NEW YORK TIMES* BESTSELLING AUTHORS, Richard and Linda Eyre were working on a set of "Joy School" lessons that parents could teach to their preschoolers. The lessons were based on the belief that rather than pushing our three- and four-year-olds academically, we should give them the greater gift of social and emotional "Joys"—core values that would help them be happy and well-adjusted when they started school and that would maximize their chances of growing into secure and productive adults.

Joy School became a worldwide phenomenon, a full preschool curriculum used by hundreds of thousands of parents who form local Joy School groups and rotate as teacher. The lesson plans are complete and detailed enough that any mom or dad can teach them, and include songs, games, activities, and stories to teach each of the twelve basic Joys.

Today, Joy School continues to expand and is completely available online at JoySchools.com and at ValuesParenting.com, where it is joined by Alexander's Amazing Adventures—a set of dramatic stories that teach values to elementary-age kids. And a related international company, Allegra Learning, teaches English as a foreign language with Joy School online games, activities, and dialogues that incorporate basic values.

Now, for the first time, Bushel & Peck Books brings together into one volume Richard and Linda's twenty-two classic children's stories from the original Joy School curriculum with new design and illustrations by Olga Zakharova. En*JOY!*

# BEN THE RICH BOY

ONCE THERE WAS A BOY NAMED Ben. He was a strong and healthy lad. But he thought he was very, very poor because he had no money. When he saw people with money and fine things, it made him want to be rich.

Ben knew that there were four very rich men in the land. One day, he decided that he would visit each of them and ask them how to be rich.

The first rich man lived in a valley in the eastern part of the land.

He was an old man with a long beard. Ben asked him how to become rich.

The old man looked at Ben and said, "How did you get to my house?"

"I walked all morning through the woods, across the stream, and over the hill," said Ben.

"Then you are rich," said the man. "You are rich because you have strong legs—you can walk and dance and skip and jump and run. I am old and lame. I would give every penny I have if I could walk like you."

Ben left the first man's house. He wanted to be rich, and if that man wouldn't tell him how, he would find someone else who would.

The second man lived on a hill in the northern part of the land. Ben asked him how to become rich.

The rich man said, "Look out my window and tell me what you see."

Ben looked out and saw beautiful red and orange autumn leaves on the autumn trees. He saw blue sky and purple, snowcapped mountains in the distance. He saw a hummingbird drinking nectar from pink and gold hollyhocks. He told the man what he saw.

"My eyes are old and tired," said the man. "You are rich because of everything that your eyes can see."

And Ben wondered why the man wouldn't tell him what he wanted to know.

Then Ben went to the third man's house, which was in a city in the southern part of the

land. The man was out on his patio. Ben introduced himself and said, "Would you tell me how to become wealthy?"

The man looked at Ben for a long time and then said, "Do you hear the crickets in my bush?"

Ben said, "Yes."

"Do you smell the food that is cooking in my house?"

"Yes."

"Then you are rich. My senses are dim. I know of the sounds and smells only because I remember them. I cannot taste, or feel, or smell, or hear as clearly as you can. If I could sense the world like you, I would gladly give every penny I have."

Again Ben wondered why the man wouldn't tell him what he wanted to know.

The last man lived in a castle in the western part of the land. Ben went to him and said, "You are my last hope. Will you tell me how to be rich?"

"But you must be rich," said the man. "Look at the fine shirt you wear."

"This?" said Ben. "I had to make this shirt with my own hands and sew it with the thread made from my sheep's wool."

"Then you are rich. Your hands can make shirts and paint pictures and play musical instruments. My hands are old and shake so much that I can do none of these things. If I could use my hands again, I would gladly give up all my money."

Ben left the man and started to go home. None of the four men had told him how to be rich. All they had told him was that he was rich already because of his body and the things it could do. As Ben walked along, the sun shone warmly on his back and he heard the birds and animals around him, and saw the flowers along his way. Perhaps he *was* rich. Maybe his body and the things it could do were worth more than money.

## QUESTIONS FOR DISCUSSION

- Why do you think the men told Ben that he was already rich?

- Look out your window with your eyes. What amazing things do you see?

- Now close your eyes and listen with your ears. What incredible sounds do you hear?

# MY BODY: TWO POEMS

By Ruth Eyre

THESE ARE MY EYES. THIS IS MY NOSE.
These are my fingers. These are my toes.
These are my ears. These are my lips.
These are my shoulders. These are my hips.

My elbows can bend and so can my knees.
I can wiggle myself however I please.
I can bend way over low or reach way up high.
I can stand on one foot as easy as pie.

I can jump up and down, or turn me around,
And if I get tired, I can sit on the ground.

*By Carol Lee Cowan*

**M**Y BODY IS THE GREATEST THING
That ever was invented!
It can't be bought, it can't be sold,
And certainly not rented.

My body has a head on top
With eyes that work for winking.
Inside my head are lots of brains
That should be used for thinking.

A nose is also on my head
To smell the lovely flowers,
And one great hole that's called a mouth
(It talks for hours and hours!).

My mouth is also useful
For something else worthwhile:
For chewing food and drinking
And a great big happy smile.

I have two arms which help me throw
And catch and lift and carry.
My arms are kind of small and thin;
My Dad's are big and hairy!

Each has an elbow all built in
To help me when I bend it.
(For folding arms to say a prayer,
I highly recommend it.)

My hands are on the ends of both
My arms, and they're exciting!
They help me do my work, you see,
Like planting peas and writing.

Two legs are on the bottom of
My body, and they're great!
Knees to help them bend and twist
I do appreciate.

My ears are on my head to hear
The sounds around me rushing.
To top it off, and keep it warm,
Is hair all soft from brushing.

Next, I have a nice long neck
To hold my head up high.
It's not as long as a giraffe's
(Which reaches to the sky!).

My feet are on the far end of
My legs, and they are fun!
They make it possible for me
To jump and wade and run.

My body is so special with
These parts, each one so fine.
The nicest thing about it is:
It's absolutely mine!

## QUESTIONS FOR DISCUSSION

- What are some of the amazing things that your body can do?

- Give yourself a big hug and say, "I love my body." How does it make you feel when you do that?

# THE PARTY

Once there were four friends. Two were girls—Saydi and Shauni—and two were boys—Josh and Jonah. At their preschool, they learned about their bodies and how to take care of them—to brush their teeth, to eat good food, and to wear coats when it's cold.

When preschool was over, Saydi said, "Don't forget to come to my birthday party on Saturday!" Then the children got their coats off their hooks and skipped along home.

Shauni hated to wear her coat though, so she just carried it along. It looked like a parachute blowing out in the breeze. By that evening, Shauni was coughing and sneezing.

Shauni remembered what she learned in preschool about taking care of her body. She put her coat on and zipped it up. That evening, her mom took her shopping to find a birthday present for Saydi.

Josh's mom reminded him to brush his teeth every morning and every night. Josh's dad always said, "Come on Josh, you can come in my bathroom and brush your teeth with me."

But Josh usually forgot to brush, or else he brushed very fast (and not very good) so he could go and play with his toys. That evening, Josh began to get a toothache.

Josh brushed his teeth every morning after breakfast and every evening before bed. That evening, when he kissed his mom goodnight, his mouth felt nice and clean.

More than anything, Jonah liked to play with cars. He knew that real cars wouldn't go unless they had gas in them. And he knew his body was a little bit like a car because it wouldn't work very well unless he put good food in it. Every day, Jonah's mom fixed good food for him to eat.

But there were lots of foods Jonah didn't like, so he left them on his plate. When he got hungry, he found lots of candy and cake. That evening, Jonah's tummy started to ache.

Jonah ate everything his mom put on his plate. If he didn't like something very much Jonah put something else in his mouth with it. That evening, Jonah's mom let him help make a birthday cake to take to Saydi.

When Saturday came, Saydi was all ready for her birthday party. She had crepe paper streamers, balloons, and a little party hat for each of her friends.

But no one could come to the party on Saturday morning. Shauni was at the doctor, Josh was at the dentist, and Jonah was home in bed with a tummy ache.

It was a wonderful party. The best part was when everyone ran around on the green grass and played "Ring Around the Rosies" with their healthy, strong bodies!

## QUESTIONS FOR DISCUSSION

- Can you find examples in the story where the children did not take good care of their bodies? What happened as a result?

- Sometimes, it can seem like doing whatever we want will make us happy. But who was happier in the story: the friends who followed the rules for taking care of their bodies, or the friends who did what *they* wanted to do instead?

- Can you think of a way you can take better care of your special body?

# Ella and Stella

**E**LLA AND STELLA HAD BEEN FRIENDS SINCE BIRTH.
Stella loved her body and Ella loved the earth.
Ella prized nature, each color and hue.
Stella admired her body and all it could do.

One day they went walking, and Ella said, "Hey!
Just look at the beauty the earth has today!
The blue sky and green grass and mountains so tall,
The sun on the back of this beetle so small!"

And Stella said, "Yes friend, those things are just fine,
But what lets me see them are these eyes of mine.
The birds in the trees and the clouds in the skies
Would mean little to me, were it not for my eyes!"

Next Ella heard crickets and birdsong above.
"Let's listen," said Ella, "to noises we love:
The sound of the brooklet and wind in the trees,
The sprinkle of rain and the humming of bees."

So Stella did listen and heard these herself.
She even heard one bird that chirped like an elf.
"I love them like you do, and every sound's clear.
But you couldn't hear any except for your ear."

Then Ella climbed up, as the steep pathway led
To the top of a hill, and to Stella she said,
"See the grass and the water, and far away snow,
And look at those flowers way down there below!"

Stella replied, "On the grass we can run.
We can swim in the water, and snow-ski for fun.
But don't forget, please, as we make our way through it,
It's our arms and our legs that allow us to do it."

They wandered back home (they had been gone for hours).
Ella gathered up pinecones and also some flowers.
"Nature's pretty and useful," she said, "and so good.
You can look at a tree, or can use it for wood!"

Stella also picked flowers and made a bouquet,
And reminded her friend for the rest of the day,
That we couldn't use wood to make lemonade stands
Or pick flowers at all without fingers and hands.

## QUESTIONS FOR DISCUSSION

- Ella loved the earth, and Stella loved her body. Do you think one is more important than the other?

- What are your favorite things about the earth? How does your body help you enjoy them?

# EARTH ERNIE

**E**RNIE WAS PLAYING ALONE ONE DAY IN HIS backyard sandbox with a little dump truck and a steam shovel. All at once he heard a whirring noise, and, when he looked up, he saw a purple, round spinning thing that looked like a big plate. Ernie knew that it was a spaceship (he had seen drawings of flying saucers in books, after all).

A hatch in the bottom opened, and out came a kid—a purple kid! Ernie knew right away that he was friendly, because he was smiling.

"Hi," said Ernie, because he was friendly too.

When the purple kid said, "Hi, Ernie," it made Ernie think of two questions. One was, "How do you know my name?" And the other was, "How do you know how to speak English?"

The purple kid said it was because he had been listening from his planet through his "ear telescope," which made faraway sounds easy to hear.

"My name is Thoyd," he said. "I came to see you because you are one of the nicest people I've listened to. I'd like you to come for a ride with me to my planet. Our king is too old to travel, and he would like to meet an Earth person."

"Well," said Ernie, "I sure would like to ride in your flying saucer and see your world, but my mom would worry about me."

"No, she won't," said Thoyd. "My spaceship goes faster than time, so I can have you right back here in your backyard before she even knows you've gone."

Well, Ernie didn't exactly understand that, and he would never have gone anywhere with a stranger who was an Earth person, but a flying saucer was something else! He climbed in.

The ride was fun. Ernie got to drive the spaceship part of the way. It had a steering wheel like a car. The ship went very fast, and once, Thoyd had to take the steering wheel because Ernie nearly hit a star.

Before long, the ship slowed down, and Ernie could see a very round, very flat, very shiny purple world. "There's my planet," said Thoyd. "Isn't it pretty?"

"Yes," said Ernie, "so shiny and flat."

"It's made out of purple plastic," said Thoyd.

"Plastic?" said Ernie.

"Yes, we made it," said Thoyd. "We used to have a world like yours, but the air and water got so dirty and there was so much garbage everywhere that we had to make ourselves this new one."

"But where are your trees and your animals, Thoyd?"

"Oh, we don't have those things anymore. They don't grow on plastic. We have synthetic food. It comes in six flavors and looks a little like toothpaste."

"But do you have any mountains to climb or lakes to swim in?"

"No," said Thoyd, "we lost those too, but this purple plastic world is great for roller skating."

Thoyd went to get the king, and Ernie looked around. The air smelled like plastic. There were no flowers or grass, no fields or hills or rocks, no sounds of birds or babbling brooks or wind in the trees. There were no farm animals or cold milk or fresh eggs, no ears of corn to pick or potatoes to dig, not even any sand or soil. The blue sky didn't look as pretty as it should next to the shiny purple horizon.

Pretty soon Thoyd came back with a very old-looking little purple man who had a purple plastic crown and a long beard. Thoyd said, "This is King Pele. He is the only purple man old enough to remember our old world, and he has a message for you."

The old king came up close to Ernie, held Ernie's hand, and leaned his mouth close to Ernie's ear. "Earth Ernie," said the old king in a gruff whisper, "tell your people to love their earth and care for it, or they will lose it just as we lost ours."

The old king patted Ernie's shoulder and smiled at him. Then he slowly walked away.

"Do you want to stay and have a tour of our world?" asked Thoyd.

"No thanks," said Ernie. He just wanted to get back to his beautiful earth to make sure it was still there.

"I understand," said Thoyd, and they got back in the flying saucer. They seemed to go more slowly on the way back, because Ernie wanted to get home so badly. Finally, they landed in his backyard and, just as Thoyd had said, Ernie's mom was still inside and everything was just as they had left it.

As soon as Thoyd was gone, Ernie ran to get his mom and his little sister. "Come on," he said, taking each of their hands.

"Where are we going, Ernie?"

"To the park," said Ernie. For the next hour, Ernie showed his mom the trees and grass and the flowers and bushes. They smelled roses, patted dogs, listened to every sound that nature made, and even picked up every scrap of litter they could find.

"We need to love our world, Mom. Otherwise, we'll lose it." Mom didn't know what had gotten into Ernie, but she agreed with him anyway.

## QUESTIONS FOR DISCUSSION

- Can you think of a way you can help take care of the earth?

# LIAM FINDS A FRIEND

**L**IAM WAS A BABY BIRD. HE had a mama bird who brought him worms to eat in their small nest in the big sycamore tree. He had learned to fly. He even had pretty red feathers. Nest, mama, worms, red feathers, air to fly in—he had everything to make him happy, right?

Then why was Liam sad? He didn't know why, but he was.

One day, another bird's nest was built on the next highest limb of the tree.

A new bird family, the Bluebirds, moved in. They had a boy bird just Liam's age named Jack. Liam and Jack flew together, played together, and explored together. Liam wasn't unhappy anymore.

## QUESTIONS FOR DISCUSSION

- Why did Liam feel different at the end of the story compared to the beginning?

- What does this teach you about friendship?

- Have you ever met someone who might be feeling like Liam in the beginning of the story? What could you do to help him or her?

# ISABEL'S LITTLE LIE

ONE DAY, ISABEL TOLD A LITTLE LIE. SHE WASN'T SUPPOSED to feed her dinner to her dog, Barker, but she did. When her mom came in and saw her plate all clean, Isabel said that she had eaten it all. (That was a little lie, wasn't it?)

The dinner was chicken, and Barker got a little bone stuck in his throat. Pretty soon he started to cough and snort and act very uncomfortable. "Do you know what's wrong with Barker?" asked Mommy.

"No," said Isabel. (That was another lie, wasn't it? But Isabel had to tell it so her mom wouldn't know she told the first lie.)

Mommy looked in Barker's mouth but couldn't see anything. "Did Barker eat something, Isabel?"

"I don't know, Mommy." (That was another lie, wasn't it? But she didn't want her mommy to know about the first two lies.)

Barker got worse, and Mommy took him to the dog hospital. Isabel went too. "What happened to the dog?" asked the vet.

"We don't know," said Isabel. (That was another lie, wasn't it? But if Isabel had told, then Mommy and the doctor would know she had lied before.)

The dog doctor said, "If it's just a bone, we could get it out with an instrument. But it might be glass, so we may have to operate."

Isabel decided it was time to tell the truth. She said, "It's a bone, and I did know Barker ate it, and I didn't eat all my dinner because I did give it to Barker, and I won't tell lies any more, because if you tell one you might have to tell more and more."

Isabel started to cry, but her mom loved her and hugged her, and Isabel decided she really would tell the truth from then on.

*Now, tell the story again, this time without the lies:*

ISABEL WASN'T SUPPOSED TO FEED HER DINNER TO HER DOG, Barker, but she did. Her mom came in and asked, "Wow, Isabel, how did you clean you plate so quickly?" Isabel knew she might get in trouble, but she didn't want to tell a lie. She told her mommy she had fed her dinner to Barker.

"Isabel, you know better than that," her mom said. Mommy hurried to the porch where Barker was and found him starting to eat

Isabel's chicken dinner. She took the chicken away before he could get any bones in his throat.

"Please don't ever give your dinner to Barker again, Isabel," said Mommy. "It can be very dangerous for him. This chicken has little bones in it that could get stuck in his throat. Thank you for telling me about your dinner. I'm very proud of you for telling the truth."

Isabel was very sorry she fed her dinner to Barker, but very, very glad she told her mommy the truth! She decided to always tell the truth from them on, and to never, never feed anything from her plate to Barker.

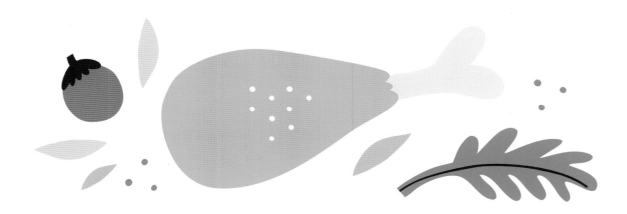

## QUESTIONS FOR DISCUSSION

- Why do you think Isabel lied to her mom about feeding Barker?

- Why did Isabel have to tell so many lies after the first one?

- Barker could have gotten very sick from the chicken bone. Can you think of other ways that our lies can hurt other people?

# ALICE LEARNS ABOUT SHARING

**L**ATE IN DECEMBER, A NEW LITTLE GIRL CAME TO ALICE'S CLASS. She was quite small for her age, and she had large brown eyes and long brown hair. Her clothes didn't seem to fit her very well and they looked sort of worn out. Her name was Emma. She sat right next to Alice in class.

The two little girls quickly became friends and one day, after school, Emma asked Alice if she could come to her house to play. Since they lived by each other and the school was just a block away, they walked home together and stopped first at Alice's house to ask her mom if it was okay. Then they went on to Emma's house.

As they walked along, Alice noticed that Emma didn't have any boots or gloves, and that her coat was very thin. She looked like she was cold and held her coat tightly around her because the zipper was broken.

Emma lived in a very small grey house. The porch railing was broken, and the paint was peeling off. She lived with her grandma, who was quite old and who looked kind of tired and worried.

Alice said, "Let's play house. What kind of dolls do you have?"

Emma said, "I only have this one doll, but you can use it and you can be the mommy." It was a small rag doll with only one arm and no clothes. Emma said, "I asked my grandma if I could have a new doll for Christmas, but she said she didn't even have enough money for food and so she couldn't buy a doll."

Alice noticed that Emma didn't have many other toys and that there were only a few clothes in her closet. She also noticed that the house was tiny and not very warm, and that the furniture was old.

Emma was fun to play with though, and her grandma was very nice.

Soon it was time for Alice to go. She said goodbye to Emma and hurried home.

Alice told her mom all about her new friend, and about Emma's cold house and her old doll and her thin coat, and that she had no boots or gloves and didn't seem to have a mom or dad. She liked Emma a lot and she kept thinking and thinking about her.

Then she had an idea. She ran to her mom and said, "Mommy, I want to give Emma one of my dolls. She could have Ellie — she's still as good as new. And she could have my blue coat. It's too small for me, but it would fit her because she's smaller than I am. And Mommy, you know that money I was saving for a bicycle? I can't ride a bike in the winter anyway. I could buy some boots and gloves for Emma. Maybe I could give her some of my old clothes, too, since I just grew out of a lot of things.

I think she would look nice in the yellow dress with the little flowers on it, and that blue sweater that's almost new."

Her mom said, "Alice, I think that's a wonderful idea. It's only one week 'till Christmas. We could wrap all the things up in holiday paper, put them in a basket, and leave them on Emma's porch on Christmas Eve. I think we should put in a gift for Emma's grandma, too." Then Mom added, "Would you like to invite them to have dinner with us on Christmas Day?"

"Oh, yes," answered Alice. "But let's leave the presents on their porch and not tell who they are from."

For the next few days, Alice and Mom were busy shopping for boots and gloves and wrapping the gifts. Mom found a very nice sweater and some slippers for Emma's grandma to go with the nice gifts for Emma.

On Christmas Eve, after it was dark, they went to Emma's house.

They quietly set the basket full of presents on the porch, knocked on the door, and then hurried away before anyone saw them.

When Emma and her grandma came to Alice's house for dinner the next day, Emma was wearing a warm blue coat with some new boots and gloves, and holding a beautiful doll tightly in her arms. She said, "Oh, Alice, just see what I got for Christmas! And Grandma got a new sweater." Then Emma took off her coat and under it she wore a pretty yellow dress with flowers on it.

Alice smiled and smiled. She felt so happy that she could hardly speak. "Oh, Emma," she breathed, "I'm so glad you had such a lovely Christmas."

## QUESTIONS FOR DISCUSSION

- What do you think made Alice the most happy: the gifts she received on Christmas, or the gifts she gave to Emma and her grandmother? Why do you think that is?

- Can you think of someone that might need some extra love or help? What could you and your family do for him or her?

# THE BEARS
# SAVE THE BABY

ONCE UPON A TIME THERE WERE THREE BEARS: A DADDY BEAR, a mama bear, and a little baby bear. One day, they were having soup for dinner and the baby bear said in his wee, little voice, "This soup is too hot."

"It is," said daddy bear in his deep, big voice. "Let's go for a walk in the woods while it cools off."

So they did. They skipped off into the woods, singing their favorite song, which was "The Bear Went Over the Mountain." When the song ended the baby bear said, "Shhh, listen—I hear someone else singing."

They all listened, and they heard a little song coming out of the deepest part of the woods. "Let's go see who it is," said the mama bear. They crept very quietly, as only bears can do.

Pretty soon, they were close enough to hear the singer clearly. His was a strange, croaky little voice, and the song went like this:

*"Today I cook, tomorrow I bake,*
*The next day the queen's child I take.*
*For she will never, never proclaim*
*That Rumpelstiltskin is my name."*

The bears got close enough to see through the trees and into a clearing. They saw a tiny, wicked-looking man dancing around his

RUMPELSTILTSKIN
IS MY NAME

fire. He sang the last line again, "For Rumpelstiltskin is my name."

In a tiny whisper, the daddy bear said, "Come this way," and the three bears walked quickly and quietly away until they could not hear the little man anymore. Then the daddy bear said in his deep, big voice, "Who was that?"

"He was bad," said the baby bear in his high, squeaky voice.

"What was he singing about?" asked the mama bear in her soft, gentle voice.

"About the princess, I think," said the daddy bear.

"He is going to take her away from the queen," said the baby bear.

"Unless the queen can guess his name," said the mama bear.

"She'll never guess a funny name like Rumpelstiltskin," said the baby bear.

"Unless we tell her," said the daddy bear.

"Let's run to the palace!" said the baby bear.

Off went the three bears as fast as their legs would carry them. At last they saw the palace. At first the guard was afraid when he saw them, but the mama bear said in her soft, gentle voice, "Don't worry, we have come to tell the queen the name of the bad little elf."

"You know his name?" said the guard. "We've all been trying to figure it out. Come with me. Right this way."

When they found the queen, she was crying and sobbing, "How can I ever learn his name?"

"We know it, we know it," said the baby bear in his high, squeaky voice.

"What? Who are you?" asked the queen, looking up.

"We found the little man in the woods," said the big daddy bear respectfully. "He didn't see us, but we heard him say his name."

The queen clapped her hands with joy, and the baby bear whispered in her ear, "Rumpelstiltskin."

That night, when the little elf showed up, laughing and thinking that he would take the baby, the bears were carefully hidden under the table so that they could watch.

"Well you don't know my name," he said, "so I'll be taking the little princess."

"Let me guess first," said the queen. "You said I had three guesses."

"All right, but hurry," said the elf. "You can never guess it."

The queen was enjoying herself now. She decided to use all of her guesses before getting it right. "Is it Jeremiah?" she asked.

"No, no, no," laughed the little man, rubbing his hands together. "Guess again."

"Is it Jehoshaphat?" said the queen.

"No, no, no, no. You'll never guess."

"Well," said the queen, "for my last guess, is it . . . Rumpelstiltskin?"

The elf turned red in the face with anger. He stomped his feet so hard that he disappeared right through the floor and was never seen again.

There was a great celebration at the palace, and the queen invited the bears to stay and to become special palace guards. The bears thanked her, but said they had to get back to their house to see if their soup had cooled off yet.

## QUESTIONS FOR DISCUSSION

- The bears might have felt a little afraid to sneak up on Rumpelstiltskin. What do you think gave them the courage to do so? How can *you* find courage to help someone in need?

# ZOUD the CLOUD

**I**N A PLACE WHERE A FOUNTAIN SPRINGS UP FROM A BOG,
The wind blew so hard it created a fog.
Then out of the fog, the wind blew a cloud.
The cloud was quite cute and called itself "Zoud."

The wind said to Zoud, as they flew from the fountain,
"Let your rain fall here, upon this high mountain.
The mountains need rain so their trees will grow tall.
If you give your rain now, it can turn to snowfall."

But Zoud shouted, "No!" He said, "No, no, no, no!
I do not want my rain to turn into snow.
I'm looking so lovely and growing so plump.
If I let my rain go, I'm quite sure I will slump."

The wind then blew Zoud over hot desert sand
(Rain is always so needed on dry and cracked land).
"Let it drip, let it drip," yelled the wind as they passed.
"It will fill up the streams; it will make the flowers last."

"Oh I couldn't, I wouldn't," Zoud said with a sigh,
"If I let my rain go I'll feel terribly dry.
Who cares about cactuses, flowers, and such?
I'd help if I could, but the cost is too much."

They came to a lake on the side of a hill.
"Come on," said the wind, "it could use a refill.
If you let your rain fall, then the lakes will not shrink,
And the people below will have something to drink."

But Zoud said, "Forget it. I'll just let them be.
Let them care for themselves, and let me care for me.
I'm so big and strong, and so fluffy and black.
Now leave me alone, Wind, get off of my back!"

The wind blew away and left Zoud on his own,
But before very long the cloud started to moan.
He felt heavy and ugly and selfish and slow;
He had no one to talk to and nowhere to go.

"I want to be happy," Zoud said, "and I thought
If I kept all my rain I would be, but I'm not.
I wonder if giving could make me feel well."
Then he called for the wind, and he started to swell.

He flew to the desert with lightning and thunder
And splashed down his rain upon all that was under.
The flowers leaped up and the brown land turned green.
Zoud felt happy and giving and no longer mean.

With a glad gust the wind pushed him on with his flight
And it lifted him high, over mountains of white.
Zoud dropped out his rain and it fell down like snow;
He saw faces so happy and smiles from below.

He was smaller and white when he came to the lake,
But he still had more water; he gave it a shake.
His rain splattered down and the lake started growing,
But all of Zoud's giving had now started showing.

Now shrunken and skinny, no thicker than paper,
Zoud wasn't a cloud; he was only a vapor.
So blowing him skillfully over the ocean,
The wind pushed him low with a powerful motion.

Zoud started to grow and replenish and build;
Water rose in the steam until Zoud was quite filled.
And he floated right off to start giving once more,
'Cause he learned a good lesson from all the before:

If you share and you give and make others feel glad,
You'll be happy yourself much more often than sad!

## QUESTIONS FOR DISCUSSION

- Zoud loved being a big, plump cloud. But the bigger he got, the less happy he felt. Why do you think that is?

- Giving to others—being *selfless*—is a wonderful way to feel joy. What is a way you can be selfless today?

# HAPPY OR SAD

**A**HMED WAS FIVE AND HAD STARTED kindergarten. He loved school, but he also loved school holidays, and this weekend was spring holiday! Ahmed's dad was taking a day off of work and Ahmed had three days off at school. He was excited! Today he was going to his friend Jimmy's to play, tomorrow Mom had promised a new toy for him and his three-year-old brother Zahid, and the next day the whole family was going on a trip to the park.

As Ahmed was walking down the sidewalk to his friend Jimmy's house, he saw his neighbor, Mrs. McGillicuddy. Mrs. McGillicuddy was old. Ahmed thought she might be somebody's grandma.

Mrs. McGillicuddy was on her porch. She was kneeling down trying to pick something up. It looked like tiny little chocolate chips, which made Ahmed think of chocolate chip cookies. Mrs. McGillicudy's shopping bag looked like it had broken, and Ahmed thought the chocolate chips must have fallen out all over the porch. It was hard for Mrs. McGillicuddy to kneel down because she was old. She couldn't find the chips very well because her eyes were old, too.

Ahmed ran on past. He was too excited about playing with Jimmy to stop and help Mrs. McGillicuddy. But when he got to Jimmy's house, he had a hard time having fun. He kept thinking about Mrs. McGillicudy and wished he had done something.

Ahmed ran over and helped Mrs. McGillicuddy pick up the chocolate chips. Doing that made him feel happy inside, and it made Mrs. McGillicuddy look happy, too. Later that evening, Mrs. McGillicuddy brought Ahmed a little basket of delicious chocolate chip cookies.

The next day, Ahmed and Zahid got their new toy, just like their mom had promised.

The toy was a long red fire engine, the kind that firemen use when they rescue a scared cat from a tree or put out a fire in a tall building!

Ahmed loved the fire engine so much that he just couldn't share it with Zahid. Zahid started to scream and cry. Then he tried to take the fire engine from Ahmed, so Ahmed pushed him and Zahid cried even louder. Their mom took the fired engine and said maybe they could have it back next week.

Ahmed shared the fire engine with Zahid. It was fun to play with it together. After he pushed it for a minute, he let Zahid push it. Zahid smiled. That made Ahmed smile. Their mom came in to watch and she smiled, too.

On the last day of vacation, Ahmed and Zahid went to the park with their mom and dad. They also brought their new fire engine and six little play cars they had gotten last year.

At the park, they met a little boy whose clothes looked a little ragged and dirty. He was nice and fun to play with. Ahmed thought he might be poor. The boy loved the little cars, especially the blue one.

The little boy looked sad when Ahmed and Zahid had to go. He didn't have anything at all to play with. When Ahmed got home, he had all his cars, and his fire engine, and all his others toys, too, but he didn't feel happy playing with them. He felt selfish.

When it was time to go, Ahmed asked his mom if he could give the little blue car to the boy, and she said that was okay.

"Thank you!" the little boy said. His face looked happy and excited—which was just how Ahmed felt!

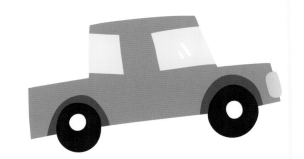

## QUESTIONS FOR DISCUSSION

- Each day, Ahmed was faced with the choice to be selfish or selfless. What decisions made him happy, and what decisions made him sad?

# JAYDEN and the MAGIC MONEY

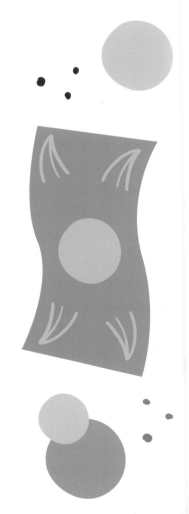

ONE FRIDAY, JAYDEN CAME HOME FROM school with a paper flyer in his hand. The paper showed a picture of a man in a tall hat and sparkly coat, holding a magic wand. Even though he was just learning to read, Jayden knew it said, "Don't Miss the Great Magenie!" because his teacher had told him all about it. Jayden's school was hosting a magic show in one week. His teacher said the magician was very famous, and the money from his show would help their school.

Jayden ran to the kitchen to tell his mom he couldn't miss the magic show. His mom said, "Jayden, we've just spent a lot of money on your birthday. If you want to go to that show, you'll have to earn enough money to buy your own ticket."

Jayden thought hard about that—so hard that he didn't even stop to eat his after-school snack. He checked his piggy bank, then went and asked his mom how much a ticket cost. She looked at the flyer and said, "Five dollars."

"I have two dollars left from my birthday money, from Grandma and Grandpa," said Jayden.

"That leaves three more dollars, then," said his mom.

Jayden went and looked under all the cushions on the couches and found four nickels.

"How many nickels is three dollars?" asked Jayden. "Sixty," said his mom. "As many as all of your fingers and toes, plus my fingers and toes, and daddy's too."

"I've got four nickels already," Jayden said, holding up his coins. His mom smiled at him and took his hand.

"Come with me," she said. Jayden's mom got a large sheet of paper and drew a big, king-size "60" on it. Then she drew a tall tower of squares by the side and wrote up the tower some numbers: 5, 10, 15 . . . all the way up to 60. Jayden got the idea before she even told him. He colored in four squares and

said, "Every time I get another nickel, I'll color another square until I get up to 60!"

"Right," said his mom, "and there are some empty water bottles in the garage that are worth five cents each at the recycling machine in the grocery store." Jayden found twelve bottles in the garage. Mom drove him to the store and watched while Jayden put the bottles in the recycling machine. He got twelve nickels and colored in twelve more squares.

"What now, Mom?" Jayden said.

"Well, I don't know," said his mom. "Can you think of any more ways to earn nickels?"

Jayden said, "More empty bottles?"

His mom said, "Sorry, that's all we've got."

Jayden said, "Maybe Mr. Johnson next door has some. I'll go see." Mr. Johnson didn't have any empty bottles, but he did have a backyard that needed cleaning, and he told Jayden he would give him ten nickels to do it. Jayden did it. Jayden kept thinking of jobs to earn nickels. By next Saturday, do you know what his chart looked like? That's right, it was completely filled in—and it was a very good magic show!

## QUESTIONS FOR DISCUSSION

- Jayden loved the magic show. Because he worked so hard to buy his own ticket, do you think he enjoyed the show even more or less?

- A goal is something we want to achieve. In this story, Jayden set a goal of earning enough money to attend the magic show. Can you think of a goal you might want in your life?

- Some goals might seem very difficult to reach. What did Jayden and his mom do in the story to make it more manageable?

- Jayden faced obstacles along the way. First, he only found a few coins under the sofa cushions. Later, he ran out of bottles to collect for the recycling machine. How did Jayden find a way through each of these obstacles?

# BREAKING AND KEEPING THE LAWS

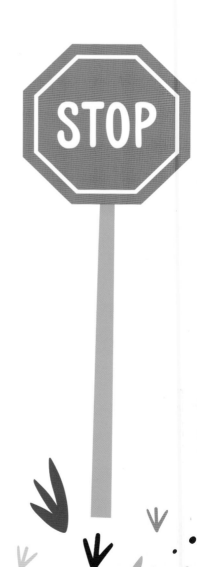

**E**li KNEW ABOUT LAWS. THERE WERE FAMILY LAWS, like going to bed on time and asking your mom before you went somewhere.

There were government laws, like paying taxes and not crossing the big street except at the crosswalk.

There were nature's laws, like the law of gravity and the law that tomatoes will only grow if you water them.

Eli knew that when you broke a law, there was a punishment.

He knew that when you kept laws, you were happy.

It was summertime. Eli was looking forward to fishing with his *zayde*—his grandpa—and to growing big red tomatoes in his garden. He thought he might even sell some tomatoes to the neighbors.

One day, mom told Eli that Zayde was coming early tomorrow morning to take him fishing. She said he would have to keep the family law of bedtime so he would be able to get up early to go with Zayde.

Eli wanted to play more than go to bed. He played with his toys until late and broke the law of bedtime. He was so tired that in the morning he woke up late, and Zayde was already gone fishing without him. Mom said maybe they could go fishing another day.

Eli kept the law and went to bed. The next morning, he got up before the sun and wasn't even tired. He caught two fish with Zayde.

It was so fun that Zayde said they might go again tomorrow.

The next day in the afternoon, Eli's friend called to ask
if Eli could come over and play.
It was a family law to ask Mom
before he went anywhere.

Eli forgot and broke the law of asking. When Zayde came to get him for fishing, Eli was gone and Mom couldn't find him. When he came home, Zayde had gone fishing without him again.

Eli kept the law and asked his mom. She said Eli could go, but only for half an hour because Zayde was coming.

Eli and Zayde went fishing again, and this time Eli caught five fish.

Eli planted some tomato plants, and Mom showed him how to water them with the red watering can. She told Eli that if he kept the nature law about watering the tomato plants, they would grow some big, red tomatoes.

Eli broke the nature law. He just got too busy playing, and most days he forgot to water those tomatoes. Some of them grew anyway, but they weren't very big or very red.

Eli kept the law. He watered the tomatoes every day and hundreds of juicy red ones grew!

Eli wanted to sell some of his tomatoes to the neighbors so he would have money to buy a new tricycle. Most of the neighbors lived across the big street. There was a government law that you could cross only at the crosswalk down the street from Eli's house.

Eli broke the law. He crossed the street . . . but not at the crosswalk. A big truck almost hit Eli. It did hit his wagon and bent it badly. It smashed the tomatoes all over the road.

Eli kept the law. He crossed the street safely and sold all of his tomatoes. With the money he earned, he bought a brand new tricycle!

## QUESTIONS FOR DISCUSSION

- Each day, Eli had to choose whether to keep or break the law. What made him happier: keeping the law, or breaking it?

# CHEEKEY AND THE LAWS

CHEEKEY WAS A BABY MONKEY. HE LIVED IN A TREE WITH HIS DAD, his mom, and his sisters. The family's tree was in the jungle. In the jungle there were some laws. They were jungle laws. Do you know what laws are? (Things that you must do right or else you get a punishment.) Do you know what a punishment is? (Something sad that happens when you break a law.)

There were two laws in Cheekey's jungle. One was that whenever you were in a tree, you had to hold on with your hand, or your foot, or your tail. What do you think the punishment was if you broke the law? (You would fall!)

The other jungle law was that if you saw a lion coming, you had to quickly climb up a tree. What do you think the punishment was if you broke the law? (You would get eaten up!)

In Cheekey's own family tree, there were two family laws. One law was that you couldn't go out of the tree without asking. Why do you think they had that law? (So Cheekey wouldn't get lost.) Why didn't his mom and dad want him to get lost? (Because they loved him.) What do you think the punishment was if Cheekey went out of his tree? (He had to go sit on the time-out limb.) Why did his mom do that? (So that he wouldn't go out of the tree again.) Why didn't she want him to do it again? (Because she loved him and didn't want him to get lost.)

The other monkey family law was to never drop your banana peels on the limbs of the family tree. Why do you think they had that law? (So that no one would slip on them and fall out of the tree.) Why did the monkey family decide to have a law like that? (Because they loved each other and didn't want anyone in their family to get hurt.) What do you think the punishment was for breaking that law? (The time-out

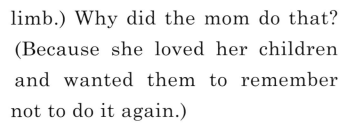

limb.) Why did the mom do that? (Because she loved her children and wanted them to remember not to do it again.)

Now I'm going to tell you the things that happened to Cheekey one day. Sometimes there were laws to tell him what to do, and sometimes there weren't any laws and he could decide for himself.

When Cheekey first woke up in the morning, he had to stretch and yawn and he almost let go of the branch. Was there a law to tell him what to do? (Yes: hold on or he would fall.)

Then he looked at his two hats: a baseball one and a cowboy one. Was there a law to tell him which to wear? (No, he could choose whichever one he wanted. He chose the baseball one.)

Next he wanted to climb down out of the tree to find a banana for breakfast. Was there a law to tell him what to do? (Yes: ask his mom so she would know where he was and he wouldn't get lost.)

He found a big banana and a little banana. Was there a law to tell him which one to choose? (No: he could choose either one he wished.) Cheekey chose the big one because he was very hungry.

While he was walking back to his tree, he saw a lion. Was there a law to tell him what to do? (Yes: climb up a tree quickly or the lion would eat him!) Cheekey climbed up a tree.

After the lion went away, he went back to his own tree and wondered which limb to sit on to eat the banana. Was there a law to tell him where to sit? (No: he could choose any limb he wanted.)

When he peeled the banana, was there a law about the peel? (Yes: don't leave it on a limb.)

Cheekey had a fun, safe day. It's fun and safe when you know the laws and do what they say, and it's fun to decide things when there isn't a law about them.

## QUESTIONS FOR DISCUSSION

- Some choices are governed by laws, while other choices are up to us. Look back at the story. Can you see examples of each?

- Think about your day today. What choices did you make that were up to you? What choices did you make that involved laws?

- Making good choices can help us feel confident and safe. Can you see examples in this story?

# Chloe's New mittens

ONE DAY, CHLOE GOT TO GO SHOPPING WITH HER MOM. WHEN they got to the big department store, Mom had an idea.

"Chloe, you need some new mittens. I'll take you over to the lady who sells them and give you some money. You can make your own decision about which mittens you want. The lady will help you while I look at winter coats just over there. I'll check on you in a half hour to see which pair you chose."

Chloe thought it was a great idea. Mom said, "Maybe you should get the kind where your fingers are all in together. They are warmer than the kind with a place for each finger, but you can make your own choice."

The lady showed Chloe all different kinds of mittens and gloves. Chloe was excited to make her own decision. She started trying them on. She tried on some that had a place for each finger, even though she knew they weren't as warm.

She tried on some very fat, fluffy, woolly ones where all but the thumb were in together.

She tried on some shiny gray and red ones that the lady said were waterproof. There were so many kinds. This was a hard decision. Then the lady had to help someone else for a minute. She said Chloe could try on any mittens that she liked.

Chloe saw some wonderful striped ones. They were very thick and woolly and warm, and all the fingers—even the thumb— went in together. She tried them on and decided they were the ones she wanted.

The lady came back and said, "Are you sure you want those, dear?"

Chloe said, "Yes, I've made my decision."

The lady said, "But Chloe, those are s—"

Just then, they heard a laugh. They turned to see Chloe's mom. She put her arm around Chloe and said, "I think you made a very interesting decision, Chloe. We'll take them—and if you ever get tired of wearing them on your hands, you can wear them on your feet!"

## QUESTIONS FOR DISCUSSION

- Chloe tried lots of different mittens before finally making her choice. What helped her make her decision?

- It turns out that Chloe picked socks instead of mittens! But rather than feel embarrassed when she found out, she stuck with her choice. Why do you think she felt so confident about it?

- What did Chloe's mom do that helped Chloe feel confident in her ability to make decisions?

# MAISY AND DAISY

MAISY AND DAISY WERE CHICKS, AND THEY WERE SISTERS. Maisy always hurried, while Daisy took her time and noticed everything around her. One day, when they were walking to school, they remembered it was their teacher's birthday. "I wish it were later in the year and the flowers were blooming," said Maisy. "We could bring her a bouquet!"

"Well, there are some flowers blooming," said Daisy. "I saw them yesterday, just down from the bridge that goes over the creek." (Daisy, you see, noticed nearly everything.)

So, off the girls went to the bridge. Maisy was hurrying to get there, but Daisy was noticing while they were walking. She noticed a big hollow tree and a red ribbon someone had dropped, and she noticed it was getting windy and cloudy.

They found the flowers and picked them. "Oh, if we only had something to hold them together," said Maisy. Daisy held up the red ribbon she had found. It was perfect. They tied the stems of the flowers together and started back for school.

Daisy was still noticing the wind and clouds, and when they came to the big hollow tree she said, "Maisy, it's going to rain. If we go on, we'll get very wet. But if we get into this big hollow tree, we can stay dry until the rain stops." It was a good idea, and that's exactly what they did.

The rain didn't last long, and they soon came out, nice and dry, with a dry bouquet of flowers and a dry ribbon. Maisy looked at her sister Daisy and said, "If it were not for you noticing everything so

well, we wouldn't have any flowers for our teacher. And even if we had flowers, we wouldn't have a ribbon. And even if we had flowers and a ribbon, they would have been ruined and we would have gotten soaked if you hadn't noticed that tree. I'm going to try and notice things as you always do."

That made Daisy happy, and they put their arms around each other's shoulders and skipped off to school.

## QUESTIONS FOR DISCUSSION

- What would have happened if Daisy hadn't been so good at noticing what was all around them?

- The world is filled with wonderful things. Take a moment to look around you. What do you see? What do you hear? What do you feel?

# LUCY'S IMAGINATION

ITTLE LUCY'S BEST FRIEND was her big sister. They played together almost all of the time! But one day, Lucy's sister got old enough to go to school, and little Lucy didn't have anyone to play with.

Lucy just wandered around the house. She felt lonely. She felt bored and a little bit unhappy.

So, she decided to have a school of her own—with her dollies. Little Lucy sat the dolls in their school chairs, and she was the teacher. She decided that using her imagination was nearly as much fun as playing with her sister!

Soon little Lucy's mommy got her another playmate. It was a dog named Bailey. Bailey watched while Lucy built towers with the blocks. Then they figured out a game. Lucy rolled a ball, then Bailey ran after it and brought it back to her. But on one throw, the ball went under the couch. The couch was too heavy to move and too low for Lucy or Bailey to reach under it.

It made Lucy a little bit mad, and a little bit sad, because that was a fun game and now they couldn't play it anymore.

Little Lucy thought hard about the problem. Bailey thought about it too.

Then Lucy had a creative idea. She got the broom from the broom closet and pushed the ball out with the handle. Bailey barked, and they went on with their game.

Mommy reminded little Lucy to put away the blocks that Lucy and Bailey had used to build their tower. There were a lot of blocks, and Lucy didn't think it was fun to put them away. She complained about it, and it seemed to take forever!

Lucy decided to use her imagination on the blocks. First, she pretended that they were cans of food and that she was a mommy putting them in the cupboard. Then, she pretended that they were fishies and she was scooping them up into her net. Before she knew it, all the blocks were on the shelf.

The next day, little Lucy's mommy brought her some paper and crayons and a coloring book. She sat down to work and Bailey curled up by her side to watch.

She colored the pictures in the coloring book, trying very hard to stay in the lines, but she kept coloring the wrong places. After she finished two pictures, it wasn't fun anymore.

Lucy decided to draw pictures of her own instead of coloring the pictures someone else had drawn. She drew a mountain and a house. Then she drew Bailey. Her pictures didn't look like the ones in the coloring book, but they were surely fun to draw. Her mother looked at her pictures and told her she was very creative.

The next day was nice and warm, so little Lucy and Bailey went outside to play. It had rained in the night and there was a nice big puddle in the driveway. It was one of the first puddles Bailey had ever seen, so he got a drink from it. It was one of the first puddles Lucy had seen, so she started stomping right in the middle of it.

Mommy looked out the window and saw her. She noticed what a wonderful time Lucy was having, but she also noticed Lucy's shoes. She wanted to be as creative and imaginative as Lucy, so she ran out and helped Lucy take her shoes off. Then she took her shoes off and stomped in the puddle with Lucy. Bailey just kept drinking.

## QUESTIONS FOR DISCUSSION

- How did Lucy's imagination make the difference between happiness and sadness?

- Think of a time you ran into a problem. How could your imagination have helped?

# CARLOS THE SQUIRREL

IN THE TREES NEAR THE TOP OF A MOUNTAIN LIVED A WHOLE city of squirrels. It was a perfect place to live, with hollow trunks for houses, lovely branches and boughs for running and leaping, and plenty of sunshine. Best of all, it was far enough up the mountain that the wolves didn't come past very often.

The only problem was that the nut trees were quite far away. Every day in the autumn, the strongest squirrels ran to the nut trees and filled up a big box with nuts. Then they dragged the box back to the trees at the top of the hill to be stored for the winter.

All the boy squirrels helped out—except Carlos.

Carlos was the smallest squirrel, and his legs were too short to go such a long way every day. He tried it once, but he couldn't pull hard enough to help very much. "Never you mind," his dad would say. "Some squirrels are fast and have long legs, and others are strong. Each one is good at something. You are good at thinking of new ideas."

It was true. Carlos did have lots of ideas. He thought he would be an inventor when he grew up. But most of his friends thought it was better to be strong and to run fast than it was to be an inventor.

One day, Carlos was thinking of new ideas, and he thought of the idea of putting wheels on the big nut box. Late that night, he made two wheels and put them on the box. Sure enough, it was much easier to pull than before when it didn't have the wheels.

In fact, Carlos could pull it all by himself! Carlos was excited, but he was so tired from thinking of the wheels that he fell sound asleep in the box.

The next morning, all the strong squirrels grabbed the ropes to drag the box to the nut tree. (They didn't even see little Carlos asleep in the box.) How easily the box pulled along! Were they stronger? No—it was those round things on the bottom. Who put them there? What were they? All the excitement woke Carlos. He popped up from the box and told the other squirrels about how he had made the wheels.

What a hero Carlos became! With the wheels, the squirrels could make six trips a day to the nut tree instead of just one. After that day, Carlos never again wanted to trade what he was good at for what everyone else was good at. And he never again wanted to be anyone but himself.

## QUESTIONS FOR DISCUSSION

- Carlos felt very different from the other squirrels, but in the end, he was able to do something no one else could. What does that teach us about the importance of differences?

- Carlos was very creative and good at coming up with ideas. How did that help the city of squirrels?

# FLUFFY NeEDS HiS FAMiLY

ONCE UPON A TIME THERE WAS A BABY GOOSE. HE WAS SO soft and so downy that he was called Fluffy. He had three brothers and three sisters, and every day he had swimming lessons from his beautiful mama. He and his brothers and sisters swam in a line behind their mama. Fluffy was fourth in the line. He always had three sisters in front of him and three brothers behind him. Each evening when they swam to shore, they saw their papa, who was finishing an extension on the family nest.

Whenever Fluffy didn't know something, he asked his mama or papa. Whenever he didn't know how to do something, they helped him. Whenever he was hungry, they caught some tasty little bugs for him to eat. Whenever he wanted to play, he played with his three brothers and three sisters. His mama made sure he was warm, and his papa made sure he was safe.

Fluffy learned that his last name was Honker. That was his parents' name; that was his family name. Fluffy was proud to have that name—proud to swim behind his mama and proud to see his papa able to do so much and fly so fast.

One day, a big storm came, and the wind blew so hard that it made big waves on the pond. Mrs. Honker started to swim for shore. Her babies followed, but it was rainy and foggy and hard to see. Suddenly, Fluffy saw a big wave rise up in front of him. He couldn't see his mama. He couldn't see his sisters. He turned around, and he couldn't see his brothers. Fluffy was alone. Fluffy was lost.

Oh, how Fluffy cried! The storm didn't last very long, but when it was over, he couldn't see his family anywhere. It was a rather big pond and all the banks looked the same. He didn't know which way his home might be.

Fluffy felt terrible. He was hungry and cold, and there was no one to feed him or get him warm. He was lonely, and there was no one to play with. He missed his family; he needed his family.

He started to wish that he had minded his mama better and been nicer to his sisters and brothers. He started looking everywhere for anyone he knew or anything he could remember.

Finally, he saw an old, ring-necked duck swimming by the shore. Fluffy had seen him before. The old duck was a friend of his mama and papa, and he had a kind face, so Fluffy swam over to him.

"Can you help me? I'm lost," said Fluffy.

The wise old duck squinted his eyes at him. "What's your name?" he asked.

"Fluffy," said Fluffy.

"Fluffy who?" said the duck.

"Ummm . . ." For just a minute, Fluffy forgot his family name. Then he remembered. "It's Fluffy Honker," he said.

"Oh," said the wise old duck, "Are you the lucky boy with the beautiful mama and strong papa?"

"Yes," said Fluffy—he was excited now.

"Are you the lucky lad with the six brothers and sisters?"

"Yes, I am, sir," said Fluffy.

The duck knew exactly where Fluffy lived, and he took him right home. Mr. and Mrs. Honker were very happy to see their lost baby. They put their wings around him and said over and over, "Thank goodness." Fluffy's brothers and sisters stood all around him and said, "Peep, peep, peep," in a very excited way.

It's very good to have a family!

## QUESTIONS FOR DISCUSSION

- Families come in many shapes and sizes, and they are one of our greatest sources of joy. How did Fluffy's family help him feel happy?

- Fluffy was proud to be part of the Honker family. What makes you proud to be part of your family?

- Can you think of ways you can love and help your other family members?

# PETER'S BUSY FAMILY

PETER LOVED EVERYONE IN HIS FAMILY. HE HAD A brother and a sister and a mom and a dad. They liked to go places together and play together and just be together.

There were some times when Peter's family got a little too busy. His dad stayed at work too long. His mom had too many errands and jobs of her own to do. And his big sister would be off somewhere with her friends. Peter knew they all still loved him, but he wasn't quite as happy in those times as when they were all together.

There were some times when Peter's family spent a lot of time together. In the summer, they camped in the mountains. At Christmas, they went shopping and sang carols. On Sunday nights, they always had family time and a treat. They had lots of traditions in their family and that made Peter feel secure.

On Monday, Peter had a bad day. He went to school in the morning and the teacher got upset at him for talking too much. He went to his friend's house after school, but the toy they were going to play with needed a new battery. On the way home, Peter tripped and skinned his knee. By the time he got to his house, Peter felt terrible.

There was no one else home. Everybody was off somewhere being busy. He went in his room and looked at a book. He knew his mom would make him feel better when she came home, but right now . . . he felt even worse.

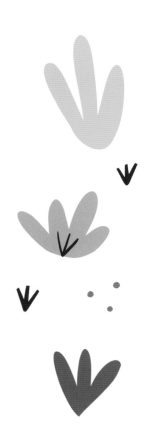

His mother came right over and put her arm around him (she could always tell when he felt bad). After he had a bandage on his knee, he ate a snack with his sister who helped put jam on his bread. He felt a lot better—and it wasn't because of the snack.

On Wednesday evening, Peter's sister had a piano recital. She had practiced hard to get ready for it because their family had a tradition of always doing their best.

Peter's sister (and his parents) wanted him to come to the recital, but Peter said he didn't want to and his parents let him stay home. After they were gone, Peter felt lonely. He felt a little bit guilty, too, because his sister had come to his soccer game last week. He wished he had gone to her recital.

Peter went to the recital. He didn't know if he'd like the music, but he knew he liked his sister. While he listened, he had a warm feeling in his heart. He felt proud of his sister and was glad that he had supported her.

On Saturday, Peter had a good day. He went to his friend's birthday party in the morning. His friend's mother said, "You remind me so much of your dad, Peter. No wonder you're such a nice boy!" In the afternoon, he got to ride his bike in the neighborhood, and on the way home, he found a quarter!

Mom and Dad had a lot of important stuff to do that evening, so they didn't have time to listen when he tried to tell them about the nice day. But Peter knew how busy they were. He went to find his dog, because he just had to tell someone!

That evening, he told everyone about the fun party and the bike riding. He showed them the quarter. His family listened to him. It looked like they were as happy as he was about his day. Sharing happy times with his family made the happy times even happier.

## QUESTIONS FOR DISCUSSION

- Peter's family made a big difference in how Peter felt each day. What were things that Peter's family did to help him feel happy? What were things that made him feel sad?

- If you were in Peter's family, what things would you want to do differently? What about in your own family?

# THe PiNG-PONG BALL AND THe CHRiSTMAS TRee BULB

ONCE UPON A TIME, AT CHRISTMASTIME, THERE WERE TWO friends. One was a Ping-Pong ball, and the other was a Christmas tree bulb.

Late each night, after the people in the house went to bed, the ball and the bulb used to talk. (They could talk to each other easily because the Christmas tree was right beside the Ping-Pong table.)

Even though they were friends, they were jealous of each other.

The Ping-Pong ball would say to the Christmas tree bulb, "Bulb, you are so lucky. You just hang there all day and people look at you and say how pretty you are. I spend the whole day getting hit with a paddle."

The bulb would say, "You're the one who's lucky. All day you get to play with the children. They hold you and pat you and have fun with you. I just hang, hang, hang. No one ever touches me or plays with me."

On Christmas Eve, when Santa came, he had one of his magic elves with him. The elf heard what the ball and the bulb were saying. He said to them, "Would you like to change places?"

They both said yes, and with one wave of his hand, the elf turned the ball into a bulb and the bulb into a ball. Just before the elf went up the chimney with Santa, he said, "The only way you can change back into what you were is to get very, very wet."

At first the bulb was happy being a ball. The children picked him up and played with him. But he got dizzy from flying through the air, and soon he missed his tree branch. He wanted to be back there, doing what he was supposed to do—hanging nice and still and looking pretty.

The ball was happy for a few minutes being a bulb. He enjoyed being shiny and bright. After a while, though, he got bored. His neck hurt from hanging on a tree, and he missed the children and the paddles. He realized that he was meant to be a Ping-Pong ball—he was good at that and not good at being a bulb.

Both of them were sad. They wanted to be themselves again. Soon they were both wishing that someone would throw water on them so they could change back. They got more and more sad. Finally,

they got so sad that they started to cry. Their tears got them very wet, and suddenly, they changed back into themselves.

## QUESTIONS FOR DISCUSSION

- What do you think the Ping-Pong ball and the Christmas tree bulb learn from their experience?

- Have you ever wished you were like someone else instead? What would you tell yourself after reading this story?

# unique
## OLIVIA

**O**NE MORNING, OLIVIA WAS SITTING on the window seat watching the rain. Behind her, in the kitchen, her mom and her mom's friend were talking to Olivia's little brother, Lucas.

"You have such beautiful blue eyes and such wonderful curly blond hair, Lucas," said the friend. People were always saying things like that to Lucas.

Olivia went into her room and shut the door. She wished her eyes were blue. She wished her hair was blond and curly. She felt sad.

Olivia went into the bathroom and looked in the mirror. She had lovely brown eyes and straight black hair that shined when she brushed it. She knew that black hair was just as pretty as blond. And she knew that no one else in the world looked exactly like her. She knew she was unique. She smiled and it made her brown eyes sparkle.

The next day, Olivia's friend, Dimah, came over. They played ball. Dimah could throw the ball better than Olivia, and she could catch it better, too.

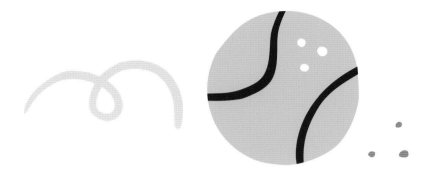

Olivia felt bad because she couldn't play ball as well as Dimah. She told Dimah that she should go home and went back in her house to play alone.

---

Olivia told Dimah that she was very good at playing ball. She watched her and kept trying to catch like she did. After a little while, they went inside together to draw pictures. Olivia was better at drawing than Dimah. She showed Dimah how to draw a puppy.

On Saturday, Olivia went to visit her cousin, Carter. Carter knew how to tie his shoelaces. When Olivia's shoes came untied, Carter said, "What's the matter, Olivia? Can't you tie your shoe?" Olivia couldn't.

Olivia felt stupid because she couldn't tie her shoe. It's hard to have fun when you're feeling stupid, so she had no fun at all.

Olivia knew why she couldn't tie her shoe. It was because no one had taught her yet. She knew that someone had taught Carter, and she had confidence that she could learn too. Olivia said, "I'm glad that you know how, Carter. You can show me!" That made them both happy.

## QUESTIONS FOR DISCUSSION

- Each day, we get to choose whether we will compare ourselves or love ourselves. What are ways that Olivia chose to love instead?

*New York Times* #1 bestselling authors Richard and Linda Eyre have written over fifty books—most on parenting, life-balance, and family—and now spend most of their time speaking to audiences around the globe and keeping up with their nine children and thirty-three grandchildren.

Olga Zakharova (a.k.a., FaveteArt) is a self-taught illustrator and letterer with two bachelor's degrees that have nothing to do with art. Olga was born in Moscow, Russia, but moved to Latvia to find some peace and quiet. She now lives in an eco-village in the forest with her husband. Surrounded by nature on a daily basis, she finds inspiration in organic shapes and the perfect imperfections of the world. Her style is a mix of playful forms and cute characters drawn by hand and then digitized. When she is not working on illustrations, she can be found sleeping or being a doorwoman for her cats.

BUSHEL
& PECK
BOOKS

Text copyright © 2020 by Richard and Linda Eyre
Illustrations copyright © 2020 by Olga Zakharova

Published by Bushel & Peck Books, www.bushelandpeckbooks.com.

Bushel & Peck Books is dedicated to fighting illiteracy all over the world. For every book we sell, we donate one to a child in need—book for book. To nominate a school or organization to receive free books, please visit www.bushelandpeckbooks.com.

Edited by Annette Sexton
Designed by David Miles

Some graphic elements licensed from Shutterstock.com: seal shape (Concentrated); emotions icons (Blan-k); mountain icon (tulpahn); speech bubble icon (CarryLove); gift icon (eViola); target icon (AlexeyYakovenko); shield icon (Belozersky); rainbow icon (senengmotret); paint icon (VolodymyrV); family icon (Serhiy Smirnov); shell icon (vectorchef).

LCCN: 2020937866
ISBN: 9781952239755

First Edition

Printed in China

10 9 8 7 6 5 4 3 2 1